THE MYSTERY OF THE FLYING ORANGE PUMPKIN

THE MYSTERY OF THE FLYING ORANGE PUMPKIN

Story and pictures by STEVEN KELLOGG

A PUFFIN PIED PIPER

To Cassie and Alexander

WITH LOVE

Brian, Ellis, and Joan bought pumpkin seeds to grow a
Halloween jack-o'-lantern. Their friend and neighbor,
Mr. Bramble, said, "Let's plant them here in my garden."

A pumpkin vine came up and blossomed. Another neighbor, Mrs. Wilkins, helped them to take care of it.

When a small pumpkin appeared, Mrs. Wilkins painted a smile on its face. The friends named it Patterson.

All summer they took care of their pumpkin and looked forward to Halloween.

"This year I'm going to be a bat," said Brian.
"I'll be a queen," said Joan.
"I'll be an alligator," said Ellis.

"I'll be a dwarf," said Mr. Bramble.
"I'll be a butterfly," said Mrs. Wilkins.

But then, at the end of the summer, Mr. Bramble
had to move away.

When Mr. Klug, the new owner, moved in, Ellis,
Joan, and Brian went to meet him. They showed him
Patterson Pumpkin.

"He's going to be our jack-o'-lantern on Halloween,"
they said.
"We'll see about that," said Mr. Klug. "I'm very fond
of pumpkin pie."

"We could have both," suggested Joan.

The next day Joan asked for permission to water
Patterson Pumpkin.
"No," said Mr. Klug. "I don't like kids running
around here."

"But the pumpkin is ours. We planted it," said Joan.
"It's on my property now," said Mr. Klug, "and it's
   going to be *my* pie!"

Joan called a meeting of the club.
"Next week is Halloween," she said, "and we're not
going to be able to carve our pumpkin."

"Maybe some Halloween tricks and treats will solve
this problem," said Mrs. Wilkins. "You kids go to town
and buy the biggest orange balloon you can find.
I'll get busy at my sewing machine."

Before sunrise on Halloween morning three ghosts and a witch crept toward Patterson Pumpkin.

They carried him away.

Later two of the ghosts slipped back with a smiling orange balloon.

The witch threw pebbles at Mr. Klug's window.

She cried, "Okitty-poppitty fiddlety-fay, pumpkin rise and fly away!"

"Police! Police!" shouted Mr. Klug.

He rushed outside. The witch and the ghosts were gone.

I can't call the police to report a flying orange pumpkin, thought Mr. Klug. They'd tell me I'm crazy!

Later that day Mrs. Wilkins telephoned Mr. Klug.
"Emergency!" she cried. "Please come at once!"

Mr. Klug ran next door.

"Here's a Halloween treat for you!" said Mrs. Wilkins.
"A freshly baked pumpkin pie!"

"We have a surprise too!" said Brian.
"A jack-o'-lantern for your front porch!"

"And here's your Halloween costume," said Mrs. Wilkins. "Step inside and try it on."